That's Love by Sam Williams and Mique Moriuchi

First published in hardback 2006
This paperback edition first published 2007 by Hodder Children's Books

Hodder Children's Books, 338 Euston Road, London NW1 3BH

Hodder Children's Books Australia, Level 17/207 Kent Street, Sydney, NSW 2000

A catalogue record of this book is available
from the British Library.

ISBN 978 0 340 91144 0

Printed in China

Hodder Children's Books is
a division of Hachette
Children's Books

For Linda, Sam, Helen and William (S.W.)   For Aki, Papa, Dan, Rich, Otti & Dave Onion (M.M.)

That's Love

Sam Williams and Mique Moriuchi

Hodder
Children's
Books

A division of Hachette Children's Books

I can name the leaves
and even the trees,
describe what I see
in the clouds on the breeze.

I can feel the air and taste the sea,

hear the buzz, buzz, buzz of a bumble bee.

Paint a colour,

smell a flower,

draw a shape,

and name the hour.

Cross the ocean, whistle a tune,

make daisy chains, and fly to the moon.

I know ALL the countries of the world

(well, at least three).

And I can count to a million
and sing doh-ray-me.

34

55

6063

623

But I can't name the look
that I see on your face.

It isn't a colour,
it isn't a place.

It's a feeling I feel,
so appealing,
so real.

Is it love?

The muddles,

A great big smile,
the softness of silence,

and all the while,
that's love.

Being kissed,

being missed,
that's love.

Wanting to share,

wanting to care,
that's love.

Knowing life is for living,

being forgiving
when it all goes wrong,
that's love.

Holding me when I cry,

helping me
to try
again,

that's love.

Seeing the good,
the way we all should.
Being special,
being there,
the way you are,
the way you care,

that's love.